KISSING A CURSE

BRITTANY LAWRENCE

AUTHOR'S NOTE

This story is set in the fictional Umbre series, following a female capybara shifter and a male chupacabra. This paranormal romance leans to cozy but has some high-stakes suspense. Please review the following before reading:

This story contains river tubing, swimming, flirtatious waitresses, a wooded chase scene, large cat attacks, mention of a firearm, discussion of injury, significant physical injury, blood, unique anatomy, cunnilingus, penetrative sex, and alcohol consumption.

CHAPTER

ONE

A sparkling unicorn should intimidate no one.

And yet, there I was.

I stared down at the app on my phone. The rainbow haired steed smiled up at me. Somehow, when Umbre creatures made themselves known after the American Government decided to tell the world aliens were, in fact, real, I thought we'd be a little more smoke and dagger. Less sparkle and rainbows.

Not that I really had room to talk as a capybara shifter. How much cuter could you get? A bunny? I'm sure there were some Irish witches, or shifters, out there that would tell me to sit down on the cute front.

Knowing all of this didn't stop my heart from racing, or my stomach bubbling like I'd eaten some bad fast food.

I took a deep breath and let it out as I tapped on the unicorn icon. I was ready to find a mate. Now that I didn't have to hide, or hide my children, I could try to meet someone; if not of my species, who would accept me. There weren't many of us capybara shifters here in North America, and going to our homeland in Brazil wasn't something I was interested in doing. It had never been home to me. But I didn't need someone like me. Just someone who would love me.

The unicorn flew around my screen to land on its terms and conditions.

"Are you looking for love? Are you willing to let magic take the reins? If so, you must be open to meeting and interacting with your match for one date. Details will be sent to you about your pre-arranged date once you've been matched.

Should you find you're not a match, you're wrong, but you can walk away.

By accepting these terms, you will not hold Miriam's Date-a-Base liable for true love's kiss or any magical experiences thereafter. We may use any photos submitted to us as marketing materials for any umbre creatures looking for love."

None of that sounded too bad. I clicked the little box to accept and filled out the quick questionnaire.

The screen exploded in sparkles and glitter. "Lucia, you've found a match!"

That was fast. I thought I'd have to fill out a more detailed questionnaire before I'd have any results.

I clicked on the pulsating heart.

"Your match, should you choose to accept, will meet you tomorrow at 10 a.m. on 5th and Yampa Street in Steamboat Springs. Please be dressed to get wet! Swimsuits and water shoes are required. A change of athletic clothes and hiking shoes are suggested, should you decide to continue on your date."

My stomach felt like it was in my butt. Okay, if we were going to be in Steamboat, we were probably going rafting or to one of the springs nearby. I'd never gone rafting before.

What was I going to wear? I hopped up from my bed and raced to my closet. Almost all of my outdoor gear was for work. That didn't sound like the best date attire.

TWO

Pushing my brown shirts aside, I found the handful of tank tops I owned. Then pulled out a teal top and pair of jean shorts and hunted for my rainbow bikini. I couldn't remember the last time I went swimming in my human form. Did I wear the swimsuit under my clothes in case things went well? Or did I wear a bra and try to find a bathroom to change?

Slipping my undershirt over my head, I swapped it for my teal tank top to see how my shirt fell over my bra. Then I stripped off my shirt and bra to put on my bikini top and put my tank top back on. It didn't have the lift my bra gave me, but I still looked super cute. I'd go with my bathing suit under my shirt. If the date didn't go as planned, maybe I could find a spot on the river to dip my toes.

I couldn't help but flex at myself in the mirror. Boy, was I sporting a serious farmer's tan from all the days of working outside. My

Brazilian heritage already gifted me with the perfect tan skin tone, but now I was a little more than sun-kissed. Probably needed to do a better job of putting on sunblock. Should I wear an over shirt?

No. He'd see my silly tan when it was time to wear my bathing suit, and I would not be one of those women who pretended to be something they weren't and hide all of their imperfections. I had a tan for goodness sake. It wasn't an imperfection; it was a sign of hard work and the love of sunshine.

I took a deep breath and took off my top and bathing suit for my oversized nightshirt. With a plan for what to wear tomorrow, I would need to leave right after breakfast to make it in time. It would be great.

THREE

I'd arrived early enough to park in a parking spot a few streets over, as far from the local businesses as I could. The parking spots near the river were already gone. The morning was still cool, but the summer sun was warming the mountain air.

Locking my car, I slipped my keys and cellphone into a plastic bag and into the zippered net bag my sister let me borrow from her kids' pool supplies. Begrudgingly, I took the sunscreen from my bag and applied it on to my reflection in my car window.

Once I'd applied more than necessary, I slipped it back into the bag and zipped it up. I gave myself one last look in the window, tightened my ponytail and started walking to 5th and Yampa.

Steamboat was just waking up for the day. The holiday crowd was already back at work. Summer vacationers would trickle in later this week, but it left the town mostly to its residents today.

The street still had holiday bunting celebrating the 4th of July. Paired with overflowing hanging baskets and stone planters lining the street full of petunias, the air smelled sweet in its summer's best.

These little mountain towns were so inviting.

At the intersection of 5th and Yampa, were two men standing in front of what looked like a shack with a large orange van waiting. The shorter of the two wore a bright yellow shirt that read, "Totally Tubers!" and swim shorts. He was holding a bright orange life jacket.

The other had blonde, shaggy hair, like back in high school when they let their hair grow out around their hat, much like it did now. He'd seen plenty of sunshine, sporting a deep summer tan. I had nothing to worry about.

"Hey! You must be Lucia." The Totally Tubers man said. "I'm Jeff, I'll be your Totally Tuber dude for the day." He handed me the life jacket. "Here is your lifejacket. I need you to keep that and your shoes on while you're on the river. It's the perfect level for a nice chill float. I got your double tube in here." He said, pointing to the orange van behind him. "Let's load up and I'll drive you to your starting destination."

The cute surfer held out his hand. "I'm Christopher, it's nice to meet you."

I took his callused hand in mine and shook it. "Lucia."

Christopher gestured to the van and held out his hand for my life vest. I handed it to him and climbed in.

"Have either of you been tubing before?" Jeff asked as he pulled us off onto the street.

Shaking my head as I slipped my seatbelt on. "It's been on the to do." I had been invited a few times, but it had been after work, and by the time I'm done working for the day, the last thing I wanted to do was get wet and have to drive home soggy.

Christopher slipped on his seatbelt. "I'm happy to be your first time."

I just smiled awkwardly, because we were already starting with the sexual innuendos. Great. Good thing I could swim should I need to ditch him.

"No worries." Jeff said. "Like I said, it's gonna be a nice chill float. No alcohol or glass on the river, but you're free to drink water. Don't suggest it from the river, though. When you come to some rocks, if you can give it a little rebound with your foot, do it. You don't wanna pop your tube before you can finish your float. Same goes for trees. Try to steer yourselves away from any wood you see. There are a few little drops, but nothing you should be concerned about. When you see the signs to exit your tube, I want you to float out. I don't want you to stand up and possibly snag your foot on something. Just slip out of the tube and swim to the bank." He pointed to Shaggy skater boy. "You hang on to the tube, and carry it to the sidewalk. I'll meet you both with a bus to bring you back up here."

We both nodded.

I was a little insulted. He wanted the guy to do the heavy lifting. I am quite the swimmer. Capybaras just are. Looking Christopher up and down, I could see why Jeff would want him to do it. Chivalry and a very large muscular build, compared to mine, did make logical sense. But I was still a little annoyed by it.

The rest of the short drive was quiet as we watched the trees pass by. The leaves were at peak green for the year. This close to the mountains, the purple from afar fractured into deep blues, blacks, grays, whites, and red. Layers of rocks built up and broke away as they became mountains, or cliff sides.

Jeff pulled us into the KOA campground, past campers, cabins and a few tents. He drove us almost right next to the river. There wasn't anyone else here yet. Which I wouldn't have guessed with the lack of parking earlier. Maybe they were done with the first float of the day.

"Groovy! I'll grab your tube and meet you next to the water."

We unbuckled our belts and slid the door open. The river almost met the edge of the road here. To each side of this gentle slope of rocks were large boulders. A group of kids were busy climbing with their fishing poles.

Christopher handed me my life vest, and I tugged it on.

Jeff set the tube down on the water at the edge of a small embankment that was easy enough to walk down. "Great day for a relaxing float down the river. Make sure to keep those life vests on until you meet land again."

Did people often try to break the rules and take off their life vest?

Christopher took the seat farthest from Jeff's hand and held onto the edge of a boulder there. "We've got you. Just sit back."

Moving my bag from my side to sit on my stomach, I turned around, and squatted back into the tube. It felt like the most unflattering position I could have been in on a first date.

I didn't know how much farther my butt was from the float when my foot slipped and I plopped into the tube. Christopher's arm grabbed my shoulders as we tipped back toward the water, but held us up.

"I've got you."

Yeah, I almost took a dunk after plopping my butt into the tube. Lovely.

Christopher pushed us away from the boulder into the middle of the river, moving his arm back to his side of the tube.

Morning sunlight flitted through the leaves. The smell of the river and the mountain air, so crisp and clean. The grass on the bank of the river smelt so delicious and fresh.

I leaned my head back on the tube and just felt the movement of the river pushing us along. The hush and gurgle of the water. The occasional bounce as we floated under the nearby bridge. I wasn't sure I had been this relaxed in a long time.

Christopher started humming to himself.

I peeked my eyes open and turned to him, head tipped back, sunglasses on under his hat, humming to himself.

"What is it you do, Christopher?"

He adjusted his hat and looked over his shoulder at the other bank. "I'm a geophysicist. It's a fancy way of saying I mostly collect and an-alyze data for environmental impacts for the company I work for." He used his left arm as a paddle to spin us around. "If we're facing this way, there are a handful of hot springs running along the river further down. I'm not sure if we'll see them while we're tubing or not."

The trees along the river were in full bloom, and there wasn't much to be seen through them. But there were breaks here and there.

"Maybe. Have you seen them before?" I asked.

"Yeah, back in college. It's cool if you like to go look at water."

"It's more than just water, though. It's warmed by magma, right?"

He smiled a quirky smile from the side of his mouth and licked his lips. "Pretty much. Either magma or from a break in tectonic plates." He pointed to the bank. "These particular springs are from tectonic plates. However, we do have one active volcano, Dotsero. That volcano is what creates the hot springs in Glenwood."

"I didn't realize we had any active volcanoes here."

He shrugged. "It's considered a moderate threat. But we have plenty of time to be notified if it were to become a problem. Nothing to worry about."

"That doesn't scare me. Dating maybe. Not gonna lie, I was a little worried when I tried the dating app I saw posted in the bathroom of a vampire bar." I said laughing.

I was excited about dating. But let's be honest, the actual ramifications of coming out to the world were long. If science stayed behind magic, we were probably okay. But the minute humans could determine who was what and where, I worried we'd be sporting stars on our arms. But then again, maybe if we mated with enough humans we wouldn't be seen as a threat any longer.

But those were inside thoughts I wouldn't allow to turn into reality by speaking them out loud. I was superstitious, and better for it. You have enough magic wielders in your family; you listen.

Christopher snapped his fingers. "Forbidden Sips, is that the bar you were at?"

"Yep, I was there for a bachelorette party. My sister suggested I try the app from the unicorn poster in the women's bathroom."

Romantic, I know. A tale to tell the grandkids.

"Was it cool? I've been meaning to check it out."

I shrugged. "Sure, if you like dark moody atmospheres. It's just a bar. The 'vampire employees'," I said with air quotes. "Were like normal kind waitstaff. Aside from a fun drink list, and some stick on teeth it was like any themed bar." What I didn't add was it had a secret floor for Umbre's I didn't get to see because, aside from my sister, everyone we went with was human. "How did you hear about the Date-a-base?"

"A friend of mine, Miriam, actually started it. Told her I'd give it a try."

"That's cool. Is she a real unicorn?"

His smile reached from ear to ear. "You better believe it."

We came to a dip in the river. The water rushed over the edge of the tube and soaked half of me in the cold mountain runoff. I squealed as we spun around as we continued down the river.

"That's chilly!" I said. So grateful for the warm summer sunlight.

Christopher chuckled deep in his chest. "I know it. I'm just waiting for it to hit me. I love that rush as you hit some rapids. This isn't quite the same but close enough. Would you ever go rafting?"

I let out a breath I hadn't realized I was holding. "Maybe?" I shook my head. "No. No, I don't think so. I've been up for certification for a while and I just can't. Don't get me wrong, I'm a great swimmer. I'm not worried about me. But there are enough fatalities every year, I just wouldn't sleep at night if I couldn't help one of my crew. Or have a rescue turn into a recovery. I know the risk is low and that our crews are great, I just can't."

Christopher slid his glasses off his face and hooked them onto his shirt. "That's okay." He reached his hand out over mine, sitting on the tube between us. "What is it you do?" He asked.

I wrapped my thumb around his hand and let him hold mine. He was so warm compared to the cold river. "Oh, I'm a Parks and Wildlife officer. Went to school to be an elementary school teacher but I was so frustrated with the workload and the lack of one-on-one attention my kiddos needed. So now, I educate people about the animals who were here before us and how to live together. I have a lot of other responsibilities too but I focus on education."

A rowdy group of early twenty somethings floated in front of us, tied up together. None of them were wearing lifejackets, and they had a tube dedicated to what I could only assume was alcohol. I had to remind myself I was off duty. If things went poorly, I'd be here to help. I didn't have to hand out tickets on my day off. And, I didn't know if it was alcohol. They could still be drinking legally. Could be soda. Right.

Christopher stuck his thumb toward the group. "You gonna get them in trouble?"

I scrunched my nose and shook my head. "I'm on a date."

CHAPTER

SIX

Christopher nodded. "What is it you like to do on your time off?"

"I like to go swimming in my family's pond. I take my sister's kids a lot. But I try to go by myself. And I knit while I binge watch tv." I rubbed my thumb over his knuckles, his hands were so soft on top for being so rough on the inside. "How about you?"

He shrugged his shoulders and held his other arm out toward the river. "This is kind of it. I spend a lot of time outdoors when I can. Hiking, skiing, rafting. If it's outside and a little bit of an adrenaline rush or pushes me physically. I'm in. But I do like a good movie night, and play video games like a normal guy. I don't have to be out doing crazy things every moment."

I could feel my lips curling into a smile. "That's good because I am a more mellow girl."

"You have to be, being a Wildlife Officer. I imagine that comes with a lot of responsibility."

Our tube spun us again, Christopher first, as

we went over a drop in the river. I bounced onto Christopher, as our tube tipped over. He rolled us back over onto my side of the tube and held on the other end until we leveled out.

"I got you." Christopher said, his smile reaching ear to ear.

It was kind of nice not having to be the one with everything together in the moment.

"That is brisk." He said, a shiver running up his back. Then leaned back into his side of the tube, turning his face toward the sun. "But it's nice."

I wasn't sure how nice being cold was, but the water and sunshine were nice in general. And I sure didn't hate his rescue maneuver. "Thank you." I said, grateful he didn't have to drag me out of the water by my life vest.

Christopher winked at me and I could feel the blush begin on my cheeks. Or maybe it was all that sunshine? Yeah, I didn't believe it either.

We stayed like that for a while, the heat sparking between us. We held hands, but I couldn't shake the feeling of his body on top of me. Each bump in the water sent a nice bit of pressure between my legs.

I nearly missed the group of teenagers mooning us as we floated by, their fishing poles abandoned by the river side.

"Were we ever that young and carefree?" I asked.

Christopher's smile slipped just a little bit. "Maybe once."

It was like the kids had somehow broken the magic spell and heat of our earlier tumble.

"What kind of shows do you like to watch when you're not climbing a mountain?" I asked.

Christopher smiled and took a moment. "Comedies mostly. But if something looks good, I'm always open to giving it a watch. You?"

"I like cooking shows and corny b rated romance movies. Especially holiday movies. I eat those up. Gets me in the mood to knit socks every time."

"Socks huh?"

I nodded. "Don't ask me to make a blanket. I don't have the patience for it. But I can make a nice pair of socks."

"My great aunt tried to get me into knitting or crochet. The one with the hook. I can do it, but a blanket is a commitment."

"Right?" I said. "Also monotonous." It was pretty hot he could crochet.

"Can be."

"You'll have to show me how to crochet, and I can teach you how to knit."

On the side of the river was a large sign that read James Brown Bridge All Tubers Exit. About a hundred yards from us, the group of people we'd seen earlier started to abandon their tubes and swim to the bank of the river where there was a nice walkway up to the street.

"You ready for this?" Christopher asked.

"Do I have a choice?" The capybara inside of me was giddy with anticipation.

He smiled wide, and put his sunglasses back

on. "Nope." He let go of my hand and turned us so we could see that side of the river. "I'll pull in the tube and meet you on the sidewalk."

We floated along just a little longer, trying to give the group ahead of us time to get their things and off the bank before we would be on top of them.

"Let's go." Christopher said as he slid off the tube.

The river was stronger in it than being on top of it. The tug of the water pulled at me as I swam to the lowered bank of the river leading to the sidewalk.

My capybara wished I'd let her out to swim. She was frustrated with the tug and pull of the life vest, and how slow I was swimming against the current. Not that she could swim much faster than I could, she just wanted to play in the water.

Mentally, I gave her a hug and thought about the pond back home, and she stopped pouting. We'd spend some time in capybara form swimming in the pond, munching on the sweet grass around its edges later tonight. Especially under the tree. My mouth watered just thinking about it.

I grabbed the other end of the tube as I neared the bank and helped Christopher lift it out of the water.

"Thanks." He said, using the handle to throw it over his shoulder.

"Of course. This was nice."

"We'll have to do it again. There are all kinds of rivers to tube down."

I stopped for a moment. He was already thinking about meeting me again. Butterflies started to flutter in my belly and I couldn't stop myself from biting my lip. He kinda liked me.

And I think I kinda liked him.

SEVEN

Just as promised, Jeff was standing outside of the bright orange van waving us down as we climbed up the sidewalk to the road.

"Hey! How was your float?" He asked as he took the tube from Christopher.

"It was great." We said, as we unbuckled our life jackets.

"Groovy! Glad to hear it." He took our life jackets and both of our phones went off.

Christopher fished his phone out of his pocket as I searched for mine in my bag.

A text message from Miriam's Date-a-Base burst onto my screen in a cloud of glitter. "You're clicking! Dry off in the van. Jeff will drop you off at Kindle Woodfire Pizza on 12th and Yampa on the river for a prepaid and ordered lunch waiting for you. I know you worked up quite an appetite!"

I looked up at Christopher. He gave me a little eyebrow wiggle. "We're clicking."

I let out a belly laugh. "Looks like we must be."

Jeff handed us each a towel, then slid open the van door. "Take a minute to dry off and hop on in."

I slung my towel over my shoulders while I squeezed as much water from my clothes as I could, then wrapped it around me like I had just left the shower.

My shoes squished as I stepped back into the van. It wasn't my favorite feeling, but they'd dry quickly being water shoes. My belt pulled down at my towel as I buckled it, leaving me a little cooler than I liked in the air-conditioned van.

Christopher slid the door closed and buckled his seatbelt next to me. He threw his towel over my shoulders and wrapped me in it. "I run warm." He said.

"Thanks." For a shifter, you would think I would run warm too. But unless I was sitting in the sun, I enjoyed being snuggled up in warm clothes. I leaned my head on his shoulder, and he wrapped his arm around me. It really was warm.

I wasn't sure if it was all the morning sunshine or how relaxing tubing had been, but I was suddenly so relaxed and cozy, and tired.

"On our right over here, we have a group of hot springs you can walk up to on the Yampa River Core Trail straight from your restaurant Bella Fiume." He turned right and parked us on the street in front of the little Italian restaurant on the water. "Here we are. I won't be waiting to take you back to where we met, but it's not a far walk. Do you need directions or can you manage with your phones?"

"We got it. Thanks man." Christopher said, leaning forward to shake his hand.

Jeff paused, and fist bumped him. "You guys have a good day."

Christopher slid open the door, stepped out, and held his hand out for me.

"Where do you want me to put the wet towels?" I asked.

Jeff smiled back at me in the rearview mirror. "Just on the floor is cool."

I unbuckled my seatbelt, unwrapped my towels and set them on the floor. Then I took Christopher's outstretched hand and stepped out onto the sidewalk.

EIGHT

It was a small brick building with about a dozen steps and a small ramp up to the front door. Their patio wrapped around the entire building with a large awning coming off the building itself. Even outside, I could smell the wood fire stove and garlic. The hanging flowers on the patio couldn't hide its earthy smell. I bet the pizza here was amazing.

We climbed the stairs, our shoes going squish as we climbed them.

Christopher held open the door, a gust of cool air hitting us as we walked through.

A tall teenager with long, dark hair pulled up into a ponytail greeted us. "Hi! Oh my gosh, are you Lucia and Christopher?"

We looked at one another and nodded. "Yep." I said.

"How exciting! Okay, follow me. We have a table waiting for you outside on the river."

She led us back through the front doors, down to the patio. The small dining area had maybe a dozen tables adorned in white table-cloths and small vases of wildflowers, over-looking the river.

"Here is your table. I'll send your server right out for your drink order."

The patio wasn't too busy as it wasn't quite lunchtime yet, but I knew this place would be packed in about twenty minutes. I was drooling over the smell of garlic in the air.

"This place smells amazing." Christopher said as he slid his cloth napkin to his lap.

I nodded, licking my lips. "Mmmhmm. I cannot wait to see what they ordered."

A short blonde stepped up to our table. "Hey! I'm Julie, I'll be your server today." She said, setting down a plate of garlic knots. "We've received your order, your pizza is in the oven as we speak. What can I get you two to drink? Don't worry about the tab, you're covered."

"I'll take a local beer. Surprise me." Christopher said.

"Same." I said. I didn't know the first thing about beer, and without a menu, I was hopeless.

Julie looked up inquisitively. "Any food allergies?"

We both shook our heads. At least for me, being a shifter came with a few perks.

"Okay, I'll surprise you with what I think you'll like just by your vibe." She smiled and turned around.

"What kind of beer do you like to drink?" I asked once Julie was out of earshot. I wanted to see what she thought was "our vibe". Sounded fun.

Christopher shrugged. "I'm not picky. I like a good variety of beers. Now salsas, I'm a bit of a snob. How about you?"

"I like a good beer. But I'm up to drinking new things. And I'm not much of a salsa girl, and I feel like I should have my Colorado card taken for not caring about green chili."

Christopher grabbed his chest and winced.

I giggled. "But I'm very picky about my Feijoada. Nothing compares to homemade and I will fight anyone on it."

"Can't beat homemade. Now the question is, what kind of beans do you like in your Feijoada? And do you add chorizo?"

I titled my head and blinked. This man knew what feijoada was? "Black beans. No chorizo. It's gotta be pork, preferably ears and trotters but if not, bacon and whatever pork you can get your hands on."

"I'll have to give it a try. When I visited Mexico one of the guys I became friends with told me I had to try it. He made his with black and pinto beans and a bunch of meat, including chorizo."

"It's definitely a regional dish. And I'm sure all of the other versions are delicious. But my Vovo has always made it with black beans and pork, so that's my Feijoada."

"So, you're from South America?"

I shook my head. "I'm American, first generation. My family moved here in the sixties from Brazil."

Christopher grabbed a garlic knot and took a big bite, and moaned.

I'd forgotten all about them. I snatched one up and joined him. The bread was so tender and melted in your mouth, full of garlic buttery goodness.

"How about you? Where are you from?" I asked, as I grabbed another garlic knot.

"Here. Coloradan born and raised."

"Nice. And you've visited Mexico?"

Julie came back to our table with two beers on a tray. She set down a darker drink in front of Christopher and a lighter beer in front of me. She pointed to my beer. "This is the local brewery's newest beer, Let Love, it's a fruited pilsner." She pointed to Christopher's darker beer. "This is Las Amantes, a Mexican style dark lager from the same brewery." She pointed her thumb behind her. "You can actually go do a brewery tour just down the street."

"Thank you, that's really cool." I said, then took a quick sip. It was light and fruity, but it didn't taste like a seltzer or a mixed drink, just a nice sweeter beer. I could dig it.

"How are we doing? Can I get you anything else while we finish your pizza?" She said as she slid her hand across his shoulders. Christopher shrugged her off as he finished a sip of his beer and shook his head.

"No." I said. "We're good." Maybe she

thought we were siblings. Or maybe she just never learned to keep her hands to herself.

She scowled at him, raised an eyebrow, and her customer service face came back on with a false smile. "Perfect. I'll be back when your pizza is ready."

Christopher took another sip of his beer. "It's not bad." He said.

"Mine's pretty good too."

He pointed back and forth at our beers. "You want to try?"

I was a shifter. I couldn't get STDs so I was totally okay sharing a drink. But if things worked out, which they were certainly off to a good start, we'd be kissing soon anyway.

His beer tasted almost nutty, but again, still very much beer. It was really good. If only she could read people beyond their beer taste.

"That's good too." Christopher said, as he leaned back in his chair. "But to answer your question, yes. I spent a semester abroad in Mexico. I ate my weight in spicy food."

"That sounds like quite the adventure. Did you visit anywhere else, or was Mexico the focal of the trip?"

His eyes grew dark. He licked his lips. "No, I actually cut the trip short and I haven't been traveling since."

"I'm sorry to hear that. But you had fun?" I asked, grabbing one last garlic knot. They were just so good.

He nodded and grabbed one himself. "Yeah.

The food was great. Saw some touristy sights, had way too much tequila, met some cool people. Met a couple not so cool people. But–" He took a deep breath. "Yeah. How about you? Have you traveled outside the states?" He stuffed his mouth full of the garlic knot in a single bite.

Frankly, I didn't blame him. They were that good.

"Nope." I said. "I have asked my Vovo to come with me to Brazil, all expenses paid for years, but she won't go back. She says it's too hard to return." I shrugged. "I've heard stories and I've written down all the places she's been so one day, when I muster up the courage, I can go see what it was like. Maybe eat my weight in food while I'm there, if it's like her cooking. Or maybe I'll be disappointed by it."

Julie walked back to our table, holding a huge pizza stand and a few plates. "Here we go. This is our Get the Garden pizza. All of our veggies in one place. Can I get either of you anything else? Another beer?"

I shook my head. "No, but could I please get a water?"

"Water, can do. You?" She asked Christopher.

"I'll take a water as well, thank you."

She nodded and made a hasty retreat.

The pizza was a nice flat crispy crust. Thinly sliced zucchini, eggplant, tomatoes, mushrooms, and artichokes over a red sauce, topped with cheese and a balsamic glaze, and arugula. It was a salad on a pizza and I was so here for it.

Christopher took the pizza server and pulled

off two slices onto his plate. He handed me the server, and I too took two pieces. I was still hungry, even after all of that garlic bread.

The crust was crisp like you can only get from a wood fire oven. The veggies melted in your mouth, with a kiss of the sweet balsamic and crisp spice of arugula. This pizza was heavenly. I didn't see us leaving a single slice.

Christopher groaned into his pizza. "Mmm. Good beer, good pizza, great company. What more can you ask for?"

"Agreed. This is turning out to be a great day."

"Yeah. It is." He said.

Julie set our water down with a splash and left.

Girl was not happy about Christopher's rejection. And he didn't seem to even notice. He was all smiles while devouring his pizza.

We sat there as the lunch crowd started filling up tables. It wasn't long before we had people sitting on each side of us.

"Do you want the last slice?" He asked.

I shook my head. As delicious as the pizza was, with all those garlic knots and a beer, my belly was blissfully full. "Go for it."

He polished off the last slice of pizza and his water, as I sat there hugging myself, trying to keep warm.

Our phones dinged again. "Lunch was a success! Grab your cars and drive to the Fish Creek Falls Trailhead. You two take a nice relaxing walk to the falls."

Christopher looked up from his phone. "Are you game for a hike?"

I nodded. "Sure, I just need to change my shoes and grab a coat."

His smile warmed his eyes. "Alright."

CHAPTER

NINE

We parked in completely different directions, but we both had maps on our phones so we would meet back up. I was so glad I'd packed extra clothes, shoes, and a thick hoodie for the ride home.

The drive there was short, but I cranked the heat the entire drive to the small parking lot at the trailhead.

When I parked, Christopher was already there, leaning against his all-terrain vehicle. I wasn't sure what it was, but it was bigger than my little car.

I paused, holding my buckle in place, wondering if I should grab my pistol from its mounted and locked case to bring with me on our hike. Christopher didn't worry me, but I'd been on a few hikes without it and had wished I'd brought it to put an animal who'd been injured out of its misery. It was my least favorite thing about my job, but I also didn't like having to let nature take its time when I could end their suffering.

It would probably be fine. This was a short hike to the falls, and if I were to find an animal, I could always come back. That and it just didn't set a good impression bringing a gun on a first date. Though, I'm not sure Christopher would have cared. He seemed like he understood what my job included.

Christopher knocked at the window. "You okay?"

I jumped, letting the belt go to snap into the window. He stepped back, and I climbed out of the car.

"Yeah, sorry. I'm ready." I said as I grabbed my water bottle.

Christopher zipped up his windbreaker to his chin. "The wind has picked up a little bit. We might get a little bit of afternoon rain. You have a rain jacket or an umbrella with you?"

I pulled my Parks and Wildlife jacket from the back seat, slipped it on, and locked the door. Taking a deep breath, I could smell the rain on the air. We might get a little bit of sprinkle, but I wasn't worried because it was a short hike. "Okay, now I'm ready."

The parking lot was pretty empty. I imagined most were down in town for lunch right about now.

"Have you walked this trail before?" I asked.

Christopher shook his head. "Nope. This is new to me."

We came up to the fork in the trail. If we went

right, we'd follow the trail to the waterfall. If we went left, we'd end up at the Uranium Mine. A much less popular trail where I could talk freely about Umbre creatures and gauge how he felt about them. Maybe even talk about being a shifter. That was, if there were no humans within ear shot.

"So, you've never been to the Uranium Mine?"

"I knew there was one in the area, but I've never been before."

I shrugged. "We had some hikers get their ribs caught on the gate a couple years back and we had to send a team up here to help get them free. Even though there are clear signs that say not to enter the mine. It's been abandoned for a while, but the bats still use it. You wanna check it out, or do you want to go to the waterfall? It's a bit more challenging of a hike, but I figure you're kind of into that." I didn't mind the idea of seeing him sweat a little.

He laughed. "I do like a challenge."

CHAPTER

TEN

We went left and walked for a while, looking at the trees, the wild columbines growing on the side of the trail. The birds sang and chirped. It really was a perfect day.

"So, Christopher. I wanted to ask you, what are your thoughts on these new Umbre creatures?" I asked.

He paused. "Um. I don't know. Seems like they could be kinda dangerous."

"But you're friends with a unicorn. Surely, they can't all be dangerous."

"You got me there. But it does hold a higher level of not knowing, ya know?"

I stopped on the trail. That wasn't what I was hoping to hear. "Well, you know there seem to be a lot of them now. Not just your stereotypical vampires and werewolves. Which seems pretty okay. What about a bunny shifter? No harm in that? Or a witch?"

What was I doing? Maybe a bunny shifter

would be chill, but any of the others could be downright terrifying.

He straightened his shoulders as he continued up the trail. "If they were smart they would stay secret. Even Miriam."

That's what I thought too. But I was so hoping I wouldn't have to. That maybe the government had done something right for a change, bringing unity to a whole other people across nations.

I mean, we did sign up for a dating app advertised to be run by a magical unicorn who may pair you with an Umbre creature.

"You think we've come across them before without knowing?"

His eyebrows shot up. "Yeah, met a chupacabra on that Mexico trip. It's the reason I came home."

I stopped. "I'm sorry, a what? You encountered a what?" I asked. I couldn't have possibly understood him. Because chupacabras were cursed. They weren't born like shifters. My Vovo told me they were the worst of demons because they were once human. Any man evil enough to be turned into one would be pure evil. Christopher was lucky to be alive.

"A chupacabra. It haunts me to this day."

I rested my hand on his shoulder. He stopped and turned around. His eyes darkened with tears he hadn't let fall. "I'm so sorry. That must have been terrifying."

He rolled his lips in on themselves and signed

out the breath he had been holding. "It was. Thanks for understanding."

"I hope any Umbre creatures you encounter in the future are of the more gentle variety."

He took a deep breath. "I just hope to steer clear from all of it." His eyes softened into a cool blue as he looked down at me. "I'm glad you're not scared of them though."

I shrugged. "Can't be much scarier than humans."

ELEVEN

Christopher pulled out his water and took a sip. "That's true enough. Speaking of humans, are you into sports?"

I took a sip of my own water, happy for the change of subject. "Playing or watching?"

Christopher snapped his water bottle closed, and I followed suit. "Both, either."

We started back on the trail

"I played basketball and volleyball in high school. Give me a ball and I am one happy critter."

"I played basketball too."

I looked up at him. "Yeah, I can see why." He was tall. And if he had been blessed with this height in high school, he would have been prime center material.

Christopher laughed. "Oh, I wish I were this tall. I was very much a late bloomer. Didn't hit my height until the last semester of high school. By then positions were placed and I was okay being the biggest guard on our team. Didn't help me any, but it was still fun. You a Denver fan?"

"Yeah, they're my home team. Even when they're terrible I'm rooting for them." Though, going to a game was more of a challenge. My inner capybara just wanted to play with the ball. Add the over stimulation of the crowd, it either took several drinks to dull me out or a lot of control. Either way, I wasn't getting to sit and enjoy the game like everyone else.

"We'll have to go to a game one of these days."

He really was looking forward to a second date. And I wasn't weirded out by it. "That sounds like a good time." Even if a little stressful.

The trail got steeper, with more rocks and roots in our way. The wild flowers were more vibrant in larger groups the farther we got from the busy trail.

Christopher stopped to take another drink of his water, and I joined him. It was easy to get distracted and forget to drink the water you brought with you.

"You see that rock up there?" Christopher said, pointing up the trail. The tree lined path evened out to a straight incline with just a few rocks in the way, leading up to a large outcrop of boulders.

"Yeah."

"Whoever gets to that rock first gets to pick out dessert."

I could feel my eyebrows rise into my forehead. This man was planning dessert tonight.

"You're on. But you do have a serious height advantage. How are we going to even the playing field?"

Christopher smiled as he nodded his head. "Okay, good negotiator, I like that. You can have a head start, or I can run backwards."

"Backwards." I wasn't sure it would slow him down much, but it would be fun to watch.

He turned around. "I'm not sure how much of a disadvantage this is, but. . ." He shrugged. "Ready?"

"Go!" I said, taking my first steps to run up the hill.

"That's cheating!" Christopher yelled steps behind me, trying to catch up as he ran backwards.

I tripped on my own two feet, giving Christopher just enough pause to pass me. "Oh, no, better dig deep and get to that rock, or I'm picking out dessert tonight."

Straightening up, I caught up to him. "Depends on what options are on the table."

Christopher shrugged. "Probably depends on the restaurant."

"What if I want to eat in?"

Christopher's eyes widened. "That's a whole other set of options."

"Then I guess I better win." I said as I widened my gate and pushed the last few feet to the large boulder.

TWELVE

Christopher turned around, opening his water and taking a deep swig. "You're diabolical."

I shrugged and took a drink myself. "Maybe, but I was serious about dessert. Hmm, now what is it I want to have?" I leaned against the rock and thought about all of my options. A thick slice of German chocolate cake sounded delicious.

Inside me, my capybara stood on her hind feet, hoping for watermelon or honeydew. Frankly, it had been so hot they also sounded tasty. "If we do dinner and dessert, I guess I will surprise you."

"Your place or mine?" Christopher asked.

"Your's."

I still lived at home and bringing a man home was a big no on the rules. With otherworldly hearing, there was no hiding anything there.

He looked down at my lips and then back up at me. "How much farther is this mine?"

"About ten minutes." I said. My voice raspy.

His thumb traced the edge of my jaw. His nose brushing my own. "I think we can spare a few moments." He said, his lips a hair's breadth away.

I reached up and met them.

His mouth fell on mine. Devouring me as if a man dying of thirst had just found water.

He dropped his water bottle at our feet. His hands tangling in my hair as his kisses crushed me against the boulder. His body was so strong and solid against me. I dropped my water bottle and let my hands explore his back as I pulled him closer to me.

I moaned into his lips. I couldn't remember the last time someone made me feel so alive.

He rested his forehead against mine.

I took a deep breath, felt the cool breeze on one cheek, his hot breath on the other.

The leaves fluttered as high pitched squeaks, almost like a bird song called back and forth to one another.

"Fuck." I whispered.

"I'm sorry." Christopher said, stepping back, putting his hands up to his side. "I'm going too fast."

I pulled at the bottom of my coat and flipped it up toward my head to make myself bigger. "It's not you!" I shouted. "You hear that squeaking? There's a mountain lion, possibly two somewhere."

Christopher unzipped his windbreaker and followed my lead as we turned in a circle, looking up into the trees, trying to see where the squeaking had come from.

"We've gotta walk nice and slow!" I yelled. Our little race to the rock was a poor choice. But hindsight was twenty-twenty.

"I'll follow your lead." He shouted back.

My heart was pounding in my chest. I was already wound up. Hearing those squeaks without seeing where they were coming from had me right on the edge.

"Hey cat! We might not see you but we hear you. Let's not bump into each other!" I shouted, as my eyes darted back and forth from the trees to the boulders.

Each step back down the trail, my legs itched to change and run. But even in capybara form, I wouldn't outrun a mountain lion. I topped out at thirty-four miles an hour if I was going as quickly as my little legs could carry. Mountain lions could coast at forty miles an hour, topping out at fifty. Not to mention they could jump and climb trees in a way I never would.

This was their forest. I didn't know where every rock and ledge was like they did.

And I couldn't just leave Christopher to defend himself against two mountain lions, even if he were a big strong man. I'd trained for this. We could handle it.

"Yeah, cat, I've squared up to scarier boars than you and won. You do not want a piece of this!" Christopher shouted behind me.

A branch snapped behind us.

"I hear you cat." I shouted and took two steps
to turn around and face the sound.

THIRTEEN

The mountain lion poised in the branches of a tree not five feet from us. Its ears twitched as its nostrils flared, scenting the air.

"I see you cat!" I flapped my arms back and forth, snapping the fabric of my coat around me as I took another step backwards. "Keep back!"

Christopher froze. His eyes grew wide, his lips a hard line as he clenched his jaw.

"Let me know if I'm going to trip on something as I walk back backwards. Walk with me, nice and slow." I shouted.

Christopher followed suit step by step, flapping his coat. "Huah! Huah!" He kept shouting over and over.

The mountain lion raised its head to make its chirping sound again.

"Behind you!" Christopher shouted.

I froze.

"Another cat?" I shouted, keeping my eyes on the cat behind him, moving down from the tree to the top of the rock we had been making out against. They didn't normally travel together, unless they were young. Even then, it was rare.

"Yep." He shouted back.

"What's it doing? The cat behind you is slowly stalking but mostly smelling the air."

Christopher swallowed. "Same."

I started jumping up and down, shouting from deep in my chest. Christopher mirrored me.

Nothing.

The mountain lion just stared back at me. Its pupils grew larger, like a house cat ready to pounce on its favorite toy.

"I'm not sure this is working!" I said.

"I think we should run for it." Christopher screamed back.

"You're not supposed to run." Once I'm a small rodent, they'll definitely want to play with me, if not eat me. My pulse thundered through my skull. "I don't think I can keep myself from running." My voice faded to a whisper.

The mountain lion's shoulders rolled as it took another step toward our left on the rock.

Christopher let go of his coat. His hands fell to rest on my shoulders. His eyes met mine. "I've got you."

"Where do we run?" I whispered, my voice all but lost on the breeze. They knew this forest better than either of us.

He smiled, his eyes bright with laughter edged in wistful sadness. "You won't."

Christopher took two steps back. He bent forward, his shirt and coat ripping off of his broad shoulders, sharp black spines protruded from his back. His face elongated almost to that of a bear, his eyes grew large, the whites gone with nothing but bright red. His mouth was a jagged mess of fangs pointing this way and that.

He stood there, a cross between a man and a monster. And yet neither mountain lion moved. Frankly, I couldn't blame them. I couldn't either.

Christopher let out a clicking screech and lunged at the mountain lion up on the boulder behind him, trying to scare it away.

It hopped back, growling deep in its chest, and hissed at him. But didn't back down. It knew it had the high ground.

Christopher let out a screech again, the clicks vibrating in my bones.

I wasn't sure which creature scared me more. The half shifted chupacabra or the mountain lion.

The sun shifted behind the clouds. The trail disappeared into shadow.

Christopher moved a fur covered arm in front of me, guiding me toward his back. The mountain lion at the bottom of the trail growled deep in its throat as it charged a few steps, rustling up dust.

The mountain lion on the rock screamed and swiped into the air toward Christopher. They were pushing us back up the trail.

I'd hiked it once.

Was it enough to run away to safety while Christopher held them off?

We backed our way up the mountain as

Christopher met them growl for growl, rush for rush.

The trail stopped being a gentle walk and became a climb. Each step grew steeper and steeper. There was no running here.

"They've got us backed against a wall. I can't climb the rest of the trail safely without watching where I step."

"Keep going." Christopher said, his voice a crackling hiss.

He lunged forward toward the lion on the trail, his left arm scooping it up into the other puma.

I didn't stop to watch the rest of the fight, and started climbing for my life.

The trail became a narrow climb between boulders. My hands slid against them as I ran. My breath became short, and I focused on controlling it as I climbed.

The screams of a small child weren't far behind me. The eerie sound mountain lions made when they were just the right distance from you. Was it a half mile, a mile?

Fuck, this was not the time to be thinking about animal facts!

At least one mountain lion had made it past Christopher.

I dug into the ground and ran as fast as I could.

The trail opened up to one side, rocks still closing me in. I wasn't far from the uranium mine now. But I was too large to slide through to the other side of the gate. And if I stopped to shift, I would be eaten. If I kept following this trail, I'd eventually run into the river, where it was just rocks.

I was going to have to leave the trail.

Taking a deep breath, I said a mental prayer as I jumped off the trail into the brush. I didn't know where I was going. But I knew once I reached the ridgeline, I could find cell towers. If I could find them, I could find a road and hopefully humans.

Ironic, I was hoping to find humans now.

CHAPTER

FOURTEEN

The brush tugged at my jacket, and I was never so happy to have the thick ugly thing on. My face wasn't as lucky, but I took the scratches as they came and kept moving.

Each step, my breath raced from my lungs. The altitude was getting to me. I needed water and my legs burned for a break.

The hair on the back of my neck stood on end. I knew it was behind me. I couldn't spare a glance or a scream, or I'd be dead.

My foot caught a rock, and I stumbled forward, half catching myself on the trunk of a tree as I fell.

"Get up!" I screamed at myself as I found my feet underneath me.

The shadows around me grew darker as the rain we smelt earlier began to fall. I kept pushing as the rain grew stronger and my legs grew weaker.

A growling scream was the only warning I got

before the mountain lion pounced. Its claws caught my shoulder, ripping into my upper back as I tried to turn toward it.

We screamed at each other as my hands slid up the soft fur of its neck. Punching and pushing it away from me.

Then it was gone.

The rain pelted against my face. I wasn't sure if it was shock or just the rain, but I was cold to my core. Could I even stand to try and run again?

The sound of clicks and hissing set me at ease, and I let my head fall back.

Christopher had found us.

FIFTEEN

Our phones started singing that light jingle from the dating app. I swear if they said we were clicking again, I might throw my phone into the woods and forget about it.

I slid my phone from my pocket; the movement sending a searing pain through my back. The app exploded in confetti the moment I unlocked my phone. A little unicorn danced around the screen, rain drops distorting the pretty design. But that meant we had cell service. We just needed to find a place to wait out the rain or a landmark for EMS to find us.

Christopher scooped me into his arms. His claws brushed the wound on my back. I gasped, and he stilled.

"Where are you injured?" He hissed.

"My shoulder and back. It's fine." I held up my phones map, a cabin we were called out to often enough. It looked like it was only a few miles away from our current location. "Do you think you can get us to this cabin?"

Christopher observed the map and looked around. "Yes. Can you wrap your arms around my neck?"

I reached up, wrapping my arms around his neck, the pain from my back throbbed. He adjusted where his arms held me, more around my lower back and under my knees. I wasn't sure if this was better for the pain, but at least I didn't have to walk. My legs throbbed, and I was just so tired.

Christopher let out a clicking shriek.

"Are they back?" I asked, my pulse in my ears. My eyes darted into the darkness over Christopher's shoulder.

"No." He hissed. "You started to doze off. Stay awake." He sniffed aggressively against my neck, and I wondered how bad my wounds could be.

I held tighter to his neck and shoulders. My face butted up against him. The short gray black fur looked coarse but was so velvety. His large fangs blocked my view forward, like lethal brush along the trail.

I wanted to run away screaming, but he'd saved me. What had he done to become a chupacabra? How evil could this man be?

It felt like forever as we walked in the cold rain. Each step sent pings of pain through my body. At this point, my everything hurt. It took all of my energy to keep my eyes open.

The cabin was lit up against the darkness.

Christopher climbed the few steps up to the cabin, opened the door, and sighed in relief.

He set me gently down on the couch and knelt by me. He peeled off my jacket, pieces of it stuck to my open wound. I couldn't stop myself from crying out. And we still had my shirt and bra to take off.

Christopher grabbed the edge of my shirt, his claws scratched at my skin as he tried to help me pull it off.

"Can you shift back?" I asked through my teeth.

"No. Not until morning. You?"

"You knew the whole time?" Here I was thinking he was human this whole time. He didn't smell or act anything but human. I could have gone forever not knowing he was a chupacabra.

"Only after I shifted. I'm human in every sense while I'm in human form."

I took a breath and did a mental catalog of how my body felt. There was no way I could shift completely. I'd be stuck like Christopher, until I had the energy to change again.

"No. I'm too tired." I said. "Fuck. Okay." I gripped the edge of my shirt and shook as I raised my arms up toward my shoulders.

Christopher took the shirt from me and ripped it off. He hooked a claw under the front of my bra and sliced through it, leaving me exposed, and I didn't even care. In other circumstances, I'd have found this incredibly sexy. This just further affirmed how little I liked big cats.

"Can you do that to the back?" I asked.

He walked around me and sliced the other two parts of my bra off of me. His breath warm against my back. It actually felt good against my wound. Christopher nudged the straps off my shoulders and let the pieces fall next to me on the couch.

"Does it look as bad as it feels?"

He growled low in his chest. "Yes."

I leaned into the back of the couch, resting my cheek on the top.

"Don't fall asleep. Use Miriam's app to request medical."

That made sense. I didn't know of any local EMS trained to deal with either of us. Now that Umbre were known, medical procedures were popping up left and right on how to manage us. Most were not trained or prepared for us. Yet.

He shrieked at the table sitting behind the couch with the medical supplies he'd found as claws slid as he tried to open a bottle of alcohol. Taking two steps into the small kitchenette, he rummaged through the drawers, pulling out a pair of rubber edged tongs.

Christopher used the tongs to pinch the large stack of gauze.

He sat behind me. I could feel the coarse gauze as he set small stacks of it along my shoulder and back. Each time I thought he'd stop, he'd add another stack further along my back. It probably wasn't great I couldn't feel everything he was doing.

He pierced the bottle of alcohol with a claw

and squirted some onto the gauze he was holding. The smell seared my nose.

"Don't think you're putting that on my back." I said, too tired to stop him.

The cold rubbed against my lower back. "I'm just cleaning around the wound."

I used the messaging feature on the app to notify the pretty unicorn we needed medical help.

"Your medical is on their way. Give them an hour. Eat and stay awake until they get to you." The unicorn's horn touched the screen, and it exploded in glitter. At least they'd be here faster than if I were to wait in an emergency room.

"They're on their way and want us to eat." I said, my eyelids growing heavy.

"We need to stop your bleeding." He said. "Take a deep breath."

I did as best I could and cried out as he pushed against me with his forearm, using the other to wrap around me.

"Sorry." He hissed. The bottom of his jaw rested on the top of my head.

"It's okay." I said through tears. "I'm just glad you were there. What happened to the mountain lions?"

"I tried not to kill them. Threw them around pretty good though."

"Thank you." It wasn't their fault for being cats and wanting to eat a rodent that smelt delicious in the wrong body. I hoped they were okay. But at the same time, if they weren't, I wouldn't have to worry about them trying to eat another round of humans.

He rested his forehead against the side of mine.

Christopher stayed there swapping out gauze and pressing into me until I wasn't soaking through them anymore. I wasn't sure if that was because the wound was healing or because I was running out of blood. Fingers crossed for the former. As a shifter, we healed pretty quickly, but we're not immortal.

He got me a glass of water with a straw. The water tasted as if it had come straight off a glacier. This far up the mountain, maybe it had.

Christopher held a chocolate bar so delicately between his claws to my mouth. It was the best cookie wafer chocolate bar I'd ever had. He was so cute and gentle despite having such an intense looking monster.

His arms were sliced up but not bleeding. The cuts looked more like he'd been attacked by a house cat. Still vicious, but not life threatening. On his left hand, one of his claws had snapped off. I hadn't noticed until now.

"Are you okay?" I asked and took another bite of the extended chocolate bar.

He nodded his head. Long black lashes blinked over his bright red eyes. "I'll be healed once I shift, in the morning."

"That didn't answer my question."

A high pitched squeal whirled from him. I was guessing he was laughing at me.

"I'm fine." He hissed.

SIXTEEN

A knock at the door stopped me from pushing.

The sudden shift of the couch when Christopher jumped up to open the door sent stars to dance over my eyes.

Christopher answered it, blocking the doorway.

"The fuck are you, man?" A deep voice asked from the door.

"What I am, hardly matters. She needs your help. Help."

It seemed like everything my Vovo knew about Chupacabras was wrong. She couldn't have known they could be this kind.

Christopher stepped aside to reveal a tall, broad, black man. His hair cut military close to his head. "I'm Andres, I'm a military medic with the Colorado Wolf Pack and an EMT for the Evergreen fire department." He knelt beside me and took medical supplies from his bag. "Can you tell me what happened? What hurts?"

I explained about the mountain lions and how I could feel some of the wounds on my back, but not all.

He ripped the blood pressure cuff off my arm as gently as he could. "Sorry about that. My native cousins were probably curious about what you are." He took a sniff of the air. "What exactly are you?" He asked as he sat down behind me. Andres pulled the gauze from my back, and I groaned as it stuck at the edges.

"I'm a capybara." I sputtered.

"I've never smelt one before. My mother speaks highly of the capybara she knew. I'm going to flush this wound with saline and pull out the debris. Then, you've got a lot of stitches coming. If I don't, you're going to have some gruesome scars, even after shifting a few times."

"Do what you need to. Who's your Mom? I bet she knows my family. I don't know of any other capybaras in Colorado other than my own."

"I'm not sure you know her." He said as he flushed the wound.

I closed my eyes and tried to breathe through the pain and not tense up. Christopher knelt on the floor in front of me, resting his head on the arm of the couch as he set his claws over my hand. It was the closest he could to holding it. He was so damn cute.

"She lives in Florida." Andres continued. "She was born in Argentina and moved to the states when she was pregnant with me. I moved here with some combat buddies of mine after my first tour. They're part of the wolf pack."

"So you're a wolf?" I asked as I stared into Christopher's eyes. They were completely red, but like ours, they had starbursts and flecks of reddish hues. So much less intimidating. Beautiful, really.

"No, I'm a Jaguar."

Christopher growled deep in his chest, and I patted my hand on his claws.

"Of course you are." I said.

"You gotta problem with Jaguars?" He asked and stopped what he was doing.

"After tonight I'm not the biggest fan of large cats." I said. "And in the jungle they eat capybaras."

He groaned and went back to work, flushing and cleaning my wound. The saline dripped down my back to the towel he'd set there. "Ya know, I don't even blame you. But I'm here to help."

"I trust you." I said. Though, I didn't have much choice. Frankly, if a unicorn said he was good, who was I to argue with such a mystic all knowing, and gentle creature?

"I appreciate that, because when we start stitchin' you up, you're not gonna like me much."

"Can you give her medication?" Christopher hissed.

Andres jumped, his eyes wide. "Fuck man, you are scary as shit! No. She'll metabolize through it too fast. She'll have to raw dog it for now. Or I can knock you out, but I can't guarantee you won't wake up in the middle of a stitch or something."

I wrapped my hand around the top of one of Christopher's enormous claws. "I'll be okay. Just, stay with me." I was at that place you get when you're in so much pain, your body protects you from some of it. You hurt, but not nearly enough. Or maybe I was secretly a badass, and I just hadn't been hurt badly enough before. Sure.

He nodded his head and rested it back on the arm of the couch, his brows furrowed in.

Andres rustled behind me, cleaning up what he'd already done and setting out new supplies. "I'm not sure how many stitches you'll need, but it's a lot. Tell me more about capybaras. You poop squares, right?"

Christopher belted out his whirling screech of a laugh again, and I fought every instinct to join him.

"No, those are wombats." I said.

"The fuck is wrong with him?" Andres asked.

"I think he's laughing." I said, fighting not to join him.

Christopher nodded and rested his head back down on the couch.

"The fuck you two meet?"

"On a dating app run by a magical unicorn." Saying it out loud sounded even crazier than it was.

"The call from my Alpha is starting to make more sense. If this is the kind of date they set you up on, count me out."

SEVENTEEN

We rambled on, making small talk as he stitched up my back, tugging at my skin. I wasn't sure if I'd ever met a local werewolf or not, but it was possible. I'd smelt wolf out on the trail working before, so it was highly possible I'd met some in human form and didn't realize it.

"All done." Andres said from behind me, taping the last bit of gauze on my back. "After some sleep and a full meal, shift tomorrow." He started to pack up his equipment and gather all the trash we'd made out of bloody gauze. "Okay monster man, you shift into a human or this how you are?"

"He has a human form." I said.

Christopher nodded.

"Cool. If it's not healed after shifting, take a shower. Just water. Then put clean gauze on."

Christopher towered over Andres as he walked him to the door. But then again, he would tower over most humans or human forms.

Andres gave a final wave and was gone.

Now I'd heal properly, and tomorrow I'd be right as rain.

Christopher handed me the remote to the television, then walked to the small kitchen. He opened the fridge and cabinets, taking stock of supplies.

I didn't even try to turn the TV on or turn toward it to watch. Though, I probably could have. Instead, I watched Christopher move back and forth in the kitchen, gingerly grabbing a plate from the cupboard with his long claws. Ripping at plastic with ease as if he were cutting it away with a knife.

He presented me with a plate overflowing with raw veggies, a whole container of ranch, and a sandwich that could feed a whole family of four. The roast beef had me salivating. My stomach rumbled, and I happily obliged it. It wasn't the dinner we'd imagined earlier, but it did its job.

Christopher stood over the sink, slipping strips of raw steak into his mouth, doing his best not to make a mess.

When he finished, he washed his claws and held the sides of his face under the water to wash the fangs that stuck out there under the water. He'd been careful enough eating there wasn't a mess, but it made sense if he'd been hunting he'd have covered his face in blood. Worst I had to worry about was grass between my teeth. Which I had passed off as salad, many times.

I stood up with my plate, and Christopher

rushed over and took it from me. "I'm okay. But I think I want to lay down and try to get some sleep."

He nodded and went about washing our dishes.

"Will you join me?"

He froze, the water running over his hands.

"It's okay if you'd rather not, or if that's too fast." I said, as I took a step back toward the bedroom door.

Christopher set the plate down, turned off the water, and dried his claws on the kitchen towel.

He towered over me higher than he had Andres. I felt so small next to him. His red eyes drilled through me. He rested his hand under mine and gestured toward the bedroom.

Christopher was quick to pull down the covers and start arranging the pillows around the bed into a T.

"We don't have to be separated by pillows." I said. I mean, I was standing here in just my pants. We were both umbre shifters of one flavor or another. Nudeness and close-ness wasn't something I was scared of.

He shook his head. "Lean over onto the pillows from your side. I don't imagine you'll want to sleep on your back." He hissed.

I slipped off my boots and let my dirty pants fall to the floor, standing there fully naked, and did as he suggested.

The pillows were so soft and fluffy. He was right. Just leaning slightly on my shoulder this way was enough to tug at my stitches. If I put my full weight on my side, I'd be miserable.

He pulled the covers over me, up to my shoulder. Then he ripped off the remnants of his pants and laid down on the other side of the bed facing me. Christopher shifted as if he wasn't sure if he should look at me or if he should turn away, but was hesitant because of the long spines on his back.

"Just get comfortable." I said. "I'm not scared to look at that big mouth of teeth."

"You sure?" He hissed.

His eyes looked at me, searching. For what, I wasn't sure. But I wasn't going to get up and run out of here screaming. So long as he wasn't a mountain lion, I think I was going to be okay.

"I'm sure." I said. "Just get comfortable."

He stood up in all his naked glory. With his pants off, I could see his legs were more muscular than before, and his anatomy was unique. Like his back, he had… spines. Or at least I thought they were spines, because he was not aroused, and frankly, I shouldn't have spent so much time looking in that direction.

I closed my eyes and took a deep breath as I tried to calm my nerves. I shouldn't be attracted to a giant chupacabra man. His human form, sure he's very handsome.

"Are you okay?" He asked.

"Yeah. I'm good." I said. Because there was no way I was going to tell him I was aroused in this moment. Though it did distract me from my back, so I wasn't terribly upset about it.

"Are you okay if I shift completely?"

My eyes flew open. "Why wouldn't I be?"

"I won't be able to talk. I'll look like a monster."

I wanted to ask him, in comparison to what? His current form? Yes, please, so I wouldn't be so sexually confused. "You won't lose your humanity while in your other form?"

"No. I'm the one in control. I just cannot talk. And I cannot turn back into my human form until the sun touches me."

"What time is it? I asked.

"Ten." He hissed.

I patted the bed on the other side of the pillows, propping me up. "Do what you need to do, to get some sleep. I just. . . I think I'll feel safer with you here. Whatever form you find more comfortable."

He nodded and bent forward. His joints popped, bones slid, and his skin stretched and shrunk as his body reconfigured itself. Christopher's face grew ever so slightly, his eyes grew a bit bigger. Tough gray hair grew out of his back next to the dark spines on his back. His fur turned ever so blue, with a slight pattern like a chain-link fence or scales.

When he finished shifting, he was about the same size as an average black bear. The spines on his back made him look larger, though.

Christopher sniffed at the bed, set his claws on the edge, and hopped up. The mattress dipped from his weight as he crawled around in tight circles, trying to find a comfortable place to lie down.

He finally found it, plopped down on the mattress, and rested his head on the pillow next to me, facing the headboard.

A red eye swiveled and looked at me. Blinking a few times with the largest lashes I'd ever seen.

"Goodnight, Christopher."

Christopher blinked slowly a few times and closed his eyes.

I did the same and let the exhaustion win.

CHAPTER
EIGHTEEN

I woke with the intense urge to pee. Blinking a few times, I let my eyes adjust to the lack of sunlight. It was still dark out. Christopher was still sleeping peacefully across from me. If he snored, I was too tired to hear it.

Slowly, I slid my arm underneath me. The stitches at my back felt like they'd rip any second. I didn't care and wasn't sure what time it was. I was through with these wounds.

Tucking my arm back under me, I rested my head on my pillow and let the shift take me over. I could feel my body do the dance Christopher had gone through earlier, if not a lot less traumatic. Shifting didn't hurt for me. It felt like a warm spring rolling over my skin until I was no longer human, and somehow a large rodent laying on my side.

I gathered my feet underneath me and hopped off the bed as quickly and quietly as I could.

My claws pitter- pattered on the hardwood as I walked over to the door. Thankfully, I was tall enough to reach the door handle, and it swung open with ease.

I could feel the sunrise in the air. The plants smelt different this early in the day. I found a tree, looked up to each of its branches and that of their neighbors to make sure there were no mountain lions lurking about. But I doubted they would have followed us after a beating from Christopher. I relieved myself behind my tree and listened to the early morning birds.

The door to the cabin creaked open. Christopher stood there as he sniffed at the air.

I trotted around the tree, my feet sinking into early morning dew. The ground felt so good on my bare feet. I sniffed at the grass there, and took a bite. It wasn't as sweet as the grass that grew around the pond in the back of our house. But it was still a nice, crisp morning snack.

Christopher sniffed at the grass by my face. I wasn't sure he'd try to take a taste or not.

He bonked my head with his chin and ran off a few passes.

Was he trying to get me to follow him?

He sauntered back, bonked me on the head again, this time racing off a few more paces.

Tentatively, I followed.

Christopher huffed, ran up to me and bonked me on the head again. This time I got the hint. He wanted to play tag!

I chased him around trees, through the bushes, tapped his tail and turned around. He was so much faster than me it didn't take but a few steps before he tapped my back with his chin.

We raced around the cabin like that until the sun started to rise.

CHAPTER

NINETEEN

Christopher collapsed in front of the door, his body stretching violently, bowing his back as his spines and fur slid under his skin. His claws and fangs shrank back. As I blinked, his human form appeared before me, panting in the morning light.

I walked up to him, tapping my face on his, trying to kiss him.

He opened his eyes. The blue glistened in the early sunlight. "You know, you are pretty cute." He said.

I tapped his face once more before I shifted back.

"I've been told." I said as I punched his shoulder. "You're not that scary in full form."

Christopher held a hand to his chest. "I'm wounded." He laughed. "But really, I'm glad my chupacabra doesn't scare you. I don't hate it. He's just kinda scary."

I shrugged. "Your half human form is scarier." I paused. "Also, somehow very attractive."

Christopher's eyes grew wide, his brows rose. "Really? You're into that?"

I shrugged. "I don't know. I'm not, not into it."

"It's the penis isn't it?" He said with a smug look.

"It is impressive." I said, as I took a quick glance down. "You're just impressive." And he was. I wasn't sure if it was the morning or if it was because he was happy to see me, or just because, but, he was girthy, in a good way. "Though, the spines are a little intimidating in your other form."

"They're not sharp, and they don't flare back." He said, eyes darkening.

I could feel my breath shorten. Between my legs began to warm. Just knowing he wouldn't hurt me was something I was excited to explore.

"If you're open to another date, I'd be interested in exploring that, one day." I said.

He reached up, brushing a piece of hair from my face, cupping my cheek with his hand. "I'm open to a lot more dates." He said as he leaned close.

I closed the distance. When our lips met, it was gentle. His hand slipped into my hair.

My hands found his shoulders and explored his lean body as we kissed.

I rolled onto my back, pulling him down with me.

"How's your back?" Christopher asked.

I shrugged my shoulders, waiting for the tug

of the stitches but they had dissolved away. "Feels fine."

"Good." He said. His next kiss crushed against my mouth. A hunger I mirrored back. I felt like I couldn't get close enough.

His fingers slipped between my legs, finding just the right spot. He slid two fingers inside me and used his thumb to find that spot again. I moaned into his mouth as I rode on his hand, clenching onto his fingers.

He kissed over my jaw, down my neck to my breasts. There he took a nipple in his mouth, sucked and nipped at it before he turned to the other. My body was electric with want, and I couldn't get enough of him.

Christopher continued on his trail down my body until he stopped between my legs. I hadn't anticipated any of this on our first date, or I would have trimmed a little, but the look he gave me before devouring my clit, while his fingers played me like a fiddle, made the thought disappear from my mind.

I was all sensation, and he knew how to play that bundle of nerves.

He kissed his way back up my body to my mouth. I could taste myself on my tongue, and I craved to have him inside me. Pushing off the ground to my right, I rolled him onto his back, my hips pinning him to the soft ground below us as I slid over him. Slowly taking every broad inch as I got accustomed to his size.

I rocked against him, setting a slow pace, his

hands gripping my hips, grinding me against him.

"God, you're beautiful." He said.

"Thank you." I whispered against his lips.

He rolled me over onto my back, spearing me again, giving my body no time to adjust, and it hurt so good. Christopher pounded into me, hitting my cervix until I was spasming around him, arching my back, groaning into his mouth.

Together we climaxed, panting as he collapsed on top of me.

He rolled off me, and we just looked at one another as the sun continued to rise.

"Hell of a first date." He said.

I had a feeling it would be my last first date.

ABOUT THE AUTHOR

Obsessed with Urban Fantasy since picking up her first Laurell K. Hamilton novel way too young, Brittany has always known she would publish her own someday. What can she say? She likes the burn slow, the spice hot, and everything with a side of mystery and violence.

Brittany lives in Colorado with her all-male family and three cats. When she's not writing, she's hanging on for dear life and doing her best at her second job, Mom.

For more information about Brittany and her books, visit her website at www.brittany lawrence.com. Be sure to sign up for her newsletter to be the first to read deleted scenes, short stories, and exclusive content plus be the first, and sometimes only, to hear about giveaways.

ALSO BY
BRITTANY LAWRENCE

Sparks to Ash

A year ago, Marie Blackwell ran from her family and the marriage they arranged for her to a man she couldn't love. Determined to be her own person, she fled Maryland to Colorado, where she found a new coven, new beginnings, and a new hope.

Baubles and Brews, her quaint little tea shop and new home, was supposed to be Marie's fresh start, but days before its Halloween opening, chaotic energy found her.

Dark magic, sabotage, and notices from the DRC about community standards will push her to use magic in ways she promised she wouldn't.

It would be a Samhain to remember.

Coming Soon . . .

Conjuring Magic

Laura Xanthos is learning the price of magic.